THE GHASTLY McNASTYS

THE LOST TREASURE OF LITTLE SNORING

THE GHASTLY McNASTYS

THE LOST TREASURE OF LITTLE SNORING

Lyn Gardner • Ros Asquith

KIDS CAN PRESS

For joint first mates, Barnacle Ellie & Sea Dog Izzy — L.G.

For Lenny "Bluebeard" Bruce and his crew — R.A.

This edition published by Kids Can Press in 2015

First published in the UK by Piccadilly Press

Text © 2013 Lyn Gardner
Illustrations © 2013 Ros Asquith

Kids Can Press acknowledges the financial support of the Government of Ontario,
through the Ontario Media Development Corporation's Ontario Book Initiative.

Published in Canada by
Kids Can Press Ltd.
25 Dockside Drive
Toronto, ON M5A 0B5

Published in the U.S. by
Kids Can Press Ltd.
2250 Military Road
Tonawanda, NY 14150

www.kidscanpress.com

The text is set in Bembo Std.

Kids Can Press edition:
Edited by Yasemin Uçar and Katie Scott
Designed by Michael Reis

Manufactured in Malaysia, in 11/2014 by Tien Wah Press (Pte) Ltd.

CM 15 0 9 8 7 6 5 4 3 2 1

Library and Archives Canada Cataloguing in Publication

Gardner, Lyn, author
    The Ghastly McNastys : the lost treasure of Little
Snoring / written by Lyn Gardner ; illustrated by Ros Asquith.

(The Ghastly McNastys ; 1)
Interest age level: Ages 7–10.
ISBN 978-1-77138-128-4 (bound) — ISBN 978-1-77138-146-8 (pbk.)

    I. Asquith, Ros, illustrator II. Title.

PZ7.G1765Gh 2015   j823'.92   C2014-902508-4

Kids Can Press is a *f,©rUS*™ Entertainment company

WARNING!

If you're
reading this
book out loud,
WHISPER
these names:
Gruesome McNasty
and Grisly McNasty.

You have
been warned.

Chapter 1

Captain Gruesome McNasty and his twin
brother, Captain Grisly McNasty, were
standing on the deck of their ship, *The Rotten
Apple*. They had just thrown their rusty old anchor
over the side of the ship, which had screeched to a
halt leaving a terrible trail of skid marks in the sea.

"Sweaty socks! What a wickedly wonderful day for gruesomeness," declared Captain Gruesome gleefully, scratching his mustache, which was home to 761 nits, 77 fleas and a ferret.

"Squeaky underpants! What a dastardly delightful day for ghastliness," agreed his brother, Grisly.

Fleas

Nits

Spurs for tormenting sea horses

Captain Gruesome got out his telescope, stroked his mustache thoughtfully and considered the treacherous rocks that jutted out from the sandbanks and formed a semicircle not far from the harbor mouth of the small village on the island shore. The village was called Little Snoring on Sea. The rocks, which rose from the sea like vicious teeth, were known locally as the Jaws.

"Interesting," he mused, "and very useful. If a ship hit those rocks, it wouldn't stand a chance. It would be smashed to pieces."

He looked delighted at the prospect.

"And if another ship was waiting nearby …"

"… it could go to the rescue of all the passengers and crew," squawked Pegleg Polly, the parrot.

"Idiot bird," snarled Captain Gruesome, swiping his fist in Polly's direction and missing. "The waiting ship could snaffle any treasure that happened to be on board and leave the passengers and crew to their grisly fate on the sandbanks as the tide rises."

"Nasty boys!" squawked Pegleg Polly, flapping her wings and lifting off her perch just in time to avoid Captain Gruesome's fist again.

The McNasty twins were the nastiest pirates

ever to have sailed the seven seas. Everyone called them "those nasty boys," except their friends, who called them Bob and Tim. They didn't have any friends though, only imaginary ones, and even they refused to play with the twins and would only play with each other.

But they did have a second mate called Mrs. Slime, who was called Mrs. Slime on account of her nose, which ran a great deal. She didn't like the McNasty twins much either, but they paid her in boxes of tissues. That was very useful because she had already used up both sleeves wiping her nose.

Tissue mountain

Tissue hill

Slime lake

Slime puddle

extra big

Captain Gruesome and Captain Grisly were so ghastly and nasty that even the fish put their fingers over their eyes and swam in the opposite direction when they saw the twins coming in *The Rotten Apple.*

The twins were the meanest of the mean, and horrible in every way. The thing that Captain Gruesome McNasty liked best was making anyone he spied doing something nice or helpful walk the plank into shark-infested seas. Captain Grisly McNasty's favorite thing was eating cold, lumpy mashed potato left over from last night's dinner. He kept it hidden in his big bushy beard just in

case he felt peckish and was more than 700 leagues from the nearest McNasty's (a fast-food chain run by distant relatives featuring those famous octopus burgers that taste of brussels sprouts with custard).

But their absolute favorite thing was TREASURE! Particularly treasure that didn't belong to them but that they could STEAL. Every night, straight after dinner, they counted all their stolen treasure. However much they had, it was never enough to satisfy the greedy McNastys — they always wanted more.

Now there were lots of things that the McNasty twins didn't like. They didn't like brushing their teeth, so they didn't brush them except on February 29, and they never ever made an appointment to see the dentist because all dentists terrified them. They loathed boiled cabbage, which they thought smelled like cats' pee (which it does, however much your mom tries to tell you otherwise). They

Best before
10/6/1956

hated doing long division, which all pirates learn at Pirate School so that they can share out treasure, because they didn't like math and they didn't like sharing. They didn't like school and school didn't like them. (The McNasty twins had been expelled from Pirate School after the first week for cutting off all the girls' braids with their cutlasses and holding the principal ransom in the art cupboard for 100 chocolate doubloons.)

The McNasty Twins' Holiday Album

Before

After (Heh! Heh!)

But there was one thing that they hated more than all these things put together and that was the thought of anybody else finding treasure because they thought that all the treasure in the world should belong to them.

Captain Gruesome and Captain Grisly, who had the *Pirate Post* delivered by carrier seagull every morning, had long read of the rumors that Little Snoring was the site of buried pirate treasure. But it had taken them months to locate the village because they had been kicked out of Pirate School before completing basic map reading, which meant they often sailed their ship around in circles for days on end.

Their steering was so awful that on their way to Little Snoring *The Rotten Apple* had sailed right through the

middle of a family of whales, scattering them
across the sea and bumping the enormous mother
whale very hard on the nose. The McNastys,
who had no manners at all, didn't say sorry to the
whale, but sailed away, laughing loudly.

Now at last they had reached their destination.
There could be no doubt that they had found the
right place because when they peered through
their telescopes they could see a sign on the
harbor wall that declared:

Excited by the prospect of being so close
to treasure, they pointed their telescopes again
toward the picture-book perfect village perched
on the tip of the shore. First they examined the
turquoise-blue harbor, the pure white sands that
sparkled like diamonds and the rolling green hills.
Then they looked at the lighthouse. Since it had
been built more than 100 years ago, the lighthouse
had prevented 345 ships and 32 rowing boats from
being wrecked on the Jaws and ending up on the
sandbanks. The lighthouse was perched high on
the hill behind the Big, Scary, Very Dark, Dense
Forest Where No One In Their Right Mind
Would Want To Go, which was a bit frightening, so
the twins stopped looking pretty quickly.

They turned their telescopes back to the little
village with its pink and white houses, the church
with its tall spire and the school.

"Sweaty socks!" said Captain Gruesome
happily.

"Squeaky underpants!" declared Captain
Grisly excitedly.

They both laughed out
loud with pleasure, a sound
so terrible that several
gulls flying overhead
fainted in terror and fell into
the sea with a loud plop.

"This must be it! At last! Our
search is over," said Captain Grisly.

"Nobody and nothing in this
sleepy little place is going to stop us
from stealing the lost treasure of
Little Snoring," replied his brother.
"All we have to do now is find
where the treasure is hidden and
we'll be the richest as well as
the nastiest pirates ever to sail
the seven seas.

"Take down the
pirate flag, Mrs. Slime,"
ordered Captain
Gruesome, "and put up
something more suitable.

We don't want anyone to guess that the McNastys are in town."

Mrs. Slime sniffed loudly but did as she was told. She knew that if she refused she would be made to walk the plank immediately, and a soaking would only make her cold worse.

"Nasty boys!" squawked Pegleg Polly.

Chapter 2

(Definitely twice as good as Chapter 1.
It must be, because my pet terrapin tried
to eat it and he is very fussy about his food
and wouldn't touch Chapter 1.)

A t the same time that the McNastys were
looking at the village of Little Snoring,
Tat was sitting in the school, sighing heavily. He
chewed the end of his pencil and ran his hand
through his hair. He looked out the window
at the dazzling sea and wished again that he
was playing on the sparkling sandy beach of

Little Snoring. Tat wiped his forehead. It was far too hot for school. He felt like an ice-cream cone that had been left out in the Sahara Desert.

Miss Green, the teacher, had given all the children some terrifyingly difficult math problems. Tat was already in deep, deep trouble with Miss Green for failing to finish last night's math homework. Tat hated math, but he always tried his best. He had tried his best on the homework but had got completely stuck on question 193. Determined not to be defeated, he had gone downstairs to ask his mom and dad for some help, but when he reached the kitchen, the door was closed and he heard the low murmur of voices.

"All I'm asking for

is some money to buy Tallulah some new shoes," Tat's mom had said tearfully. Tallulah was Tat's little sister. "She outgrew her last pair months ago. She's been complaining for weeks that she can barely walk in them."

"I'm sorry, my darling," said Tat's dad, "but we can't afford new shoes. Our situation is quite hopeless. Since the harbor master said that machines are cheaper than people and I lost my job as the lighthouse keeper, there has been so little money coming in. I saw our landlord this morning. We're six weeks behind with the rent. Unless we can come up with the money by Monday, we'll be evicted from the house."

Tat's mom had burst into tears. Tat's heart had lurched. They were going to be forced to leave the home where he and his little sister had been born and lived their whole lives. All thought of math homework had flown straight out of his head as he'd desperately tried to come up with a plan to help his mom and dad. He had tossed and turned all night with worry.

In the morning, Tat's mom had been very pale and over breakfast she said to her husband, "There is only one thing to do, dear. We will have to row to the mainland tomorrow morning and sell my wedding ring."

Tat's dad was appalled. "I won't let you. It won't raise enough money and it means too much to us both."

Tat's mom shook her head sadly. "We can't eat gold."

Tat's dad had hugged his wife, and Tat had said, "You can have all the money in my piggy bank."

Tat's parents had hugged him hard, too.

"I'm afraid it won't be nearly enough, Tat," said his dad, "but it's kind of you to offer. The way you can help is to stay with Aunt Tessie tomorrow night while your mom and I go with Tallulah to the mainland and try to sell the ring. Maybe it will be worth more than we think and cover our debts. Then we can buy some shoes for Tallulah."

Aware of Miss Green's eyes now burning holes in him, Tat looked down again at the math problems in front of him. His head hurt. The problems were impossible.

Tat wasn't stupid, he just wasn't good at school things — he was brave as a ~~lobster~~ lion and brilliant at drawing tractors and dinosaurs, climbing trees, rowing boats, swimming underwater and eating jam sandwiches.

Tat — in case you've been wondering, and I can hardly blame you if you have — was short for Trevor Augustus Trout, which is a perfectly good name for a fishmonger or a bank manager but is a perfectly ridiculous name for a ten-year-old boy with a snub nose who is very brave and likes jam sandwiches.

He looked longingly over at his best friend Hetty. Hetty, who was the cleverest girl in the school and quite possibly the entire world, had already finished all her work and was sitting quietly reading a book called *Six Impossible Things before Breakfast: A Practical Guide for Young Overachievers*. If only Hetty was sitting next to him, she would have helped Tat by explaining very carefully what he had to do, because Tat and Hetty were best friends. Hetty was very good at explaining — much better than Miss Green who was often rather cross with everybody and always very cross with Tat. If Hetty was his teacher, he knew that he would have lots of Super Stars, but he

hadn't had a single one. Ever. It was
so unfair! Hetty looked
up from her book and
winked at Tat.

Tat grinned at her
and pulled a copy of
the *Little Snoring Gazette*
out of his bag and unfolded it
carefully under the desk. He couldn't wait to show
it to Hetty. Tat was only mildly interested in the
headline, which screamed in big black letters:

But he was very interested in a much smaller headline at the bottom of page three.

He scanned the story below that told how an old treasure map had been found in an ancient book in the Greater Snoring library and confirmed the rumors that the lost treasure of the notorious pirate Captain Syd was buried somewhere in Little Snoring. Unfortunately the map was so old and so faded that it was impossible to see exactly where X marked the spot, but experts who had examined the map had declared it genuine and believed that the lost treasure was likely to be buried on the beach.

The University of Greater Snoring was offering a generous reward to anyone who found it, although one of the experts had said that after being buried for four hundred years, it was unlikely that the treasure would ever be discovered.

Tat smiled to himself. The expert had no idea just how determined Tat could be. He knew that when he explained that his family might lose their house unless they found the treasure, Hetty would help him with the digging. They would find it, even if they had to dig all weekend.

Tat heard a meow at the window. It was his cat, who was called Dog.

Dog, who was of no particular make of cat but many makes all rolled into one, was called Dog because he thought like a dog and behaved like a dog, even though he looked and sounded like a cat.

Dog meowed loudly again and scratched at the window to get Tat's attention. Tat glanced out the window. In the distance he could see a ship had put down anchor far off the shore. Unlike his math skills, Tat's eyesight was very good. This was because he ate six carrots every morning before breakfast, which lots of people, including Hetty, would find completely impossible but Tat found easy. His eyesight was so good that he could just make out the skull and crossbones flag at the top of the ship's mast. He could also see a woman climbing the mast, wiping her nose on her sleeve as she headed upward toward the flag.

A skull and crossbones! It could mean only one thing. Pirates! Maybe they had heard about the treasure, too. Tat gasped.

Everyone in the class turned to look at him.

"What is it now, Tat?" asked Miss Green impatiently.

Tat pointed out the window toward the sea. Dog, who had cat's eyes and could see

everything, raised
a paw and pointed,
too. Dog's paw
was shaking with
fear.

Everyone
looked, but none
of them saw,
because they
didn't eat six
carrots before
breakfast every
single day.

Miss Green turned to Tat and said very sternly, "Silly boy! It's just a friendly ship paying our lovely island a visit."

"But … but … but," said Tat, "it's flying a skull and crossbones!"

"You need to eat more carrots and get your eyesight checked," said Miss Green. "Tat, you've got more imagination than brains, and if there's one thing I can't bear in my classroom it's imagination. Go and stand in the corner for the rest of the lesson." With that she pulled down the blind on the window and gave the children another math problem that was so hard that everyone's brain except Hetty's overheated.

Chapter 3

The next morning Tat went with his dad to leave his toothbrush and pajamas at Aunt Tessie's house and then went down to the harbor to say goodbye to his parents and sister before they set off in their rowing boat to the mainland.

"Remember to brush your teeth very well tonight, Tat, because Aunt Tessie will check they

are sparkling," said his dad, giving Tat a big hug.

Tat nodded. Aunt Tessie was the Little Snoring dentist and it was a matter of honor with her that no member of the Trout family ever needed a filling or believed in the tooth fairy.

"We'll row back tomorrow morning before breakfast. We'll bring jam donuts if our mission is a success," said his mom. "We love you, Tat."

When his family's rowing boat was just a speck on the horizon, Tat ran to Hetty's house and the two of them headed for the beach with spades borrowed from Hetty's garden shed. Tat had shown Hetty the newspaper article and Hetty had promised to devote the entire weekend to helping Tat look for Captain Syd's lost treasure.

Hetty was limping a little because she was wearing odd shoes. In fact, since a shoe thief had started stealing shoes from houses in the village a few months before, many of the Little Snoring

villagers — including Hetty — had to wear odd shoes every day. This was extremely inconvenient when you were trying to jump or dance or were running for the bus. (You always had to run for the bus in Little Snoring because it didn't actually stop there, it just slowed down a little.)

The strange thing about the Little Snoring shoe thief was that he or she only seemed to ever steal one shoe from every pair. It was very mysterious and extremely vexing. Hetty's mom had been forced to compete in the Little Snoring

Ballroom Dancing Championships wearing one gold sandal and a rain boot and as a result had only just scraped through to the finals.

Digging for treasure proved to be exhausting work, and the children got hot very quickly.

Tat stopped to unwrap one of several packets of jam sandwiches that he kept in his pockets. His mom always wrapped his sandwiches in the old shipping reports that had been sent to his dad when he had been the lighthouse keeper. This one was from ages ago and read:

OFFICIAL   9th JULY 1999
Expect ship bearing precious cargo to arrive
at Little Snoring tonight.

Tat folded the paper and put it carefully in his pocket to avoid littering the beach. He took a big bite from his sandwich and peered into the hole, which was now very deep.

"Some people say that if you dig deep enough, you'll eventually get to Australia," said Tat.

"Some people are wrong," said Hetty firmly.

Tat wiped the sweat off his face. "I don't think there is any treasure buried here," he said sadly. "Maybe we should try somewhere else."

To cheer himself up, Tat took another huge bite out of his jam sandwich and a splotch of jam fell to the bottom of page 39 where it made a very sticky mess.

Tat and Hetty started to dig another hole farther down the beach, and then another. Soon the beach was covered with holes!

"Maybe the treasure isn't even on the beach," said Hetty. And then her spade hit something hard.

Tat leaped into the hole and smoothed away the sand from the top of a large wooden box. "TREASURE!" he shouted at the top of his voice.

The word *treasure* carried on the wind all the way to the deck of *The Rotten Apple*, and as soon as the McNasty twins heard the word they both grinned. It was such a terrifying sight that it made

Mrs. Slime feel quite faint and her nose dripped twice as fast as the usual 2.7 miles per hour.

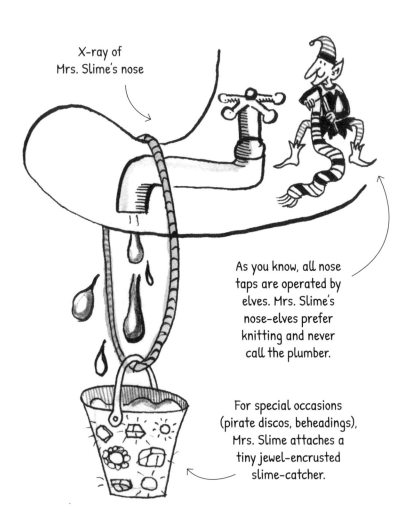

X-ray of Mrs. Slime's nose

As you know, all nose taps are operated by elves. Mrs. Slime's nose-elves prefer knitting and never call the plumber.

For special occasions (pirate discos, beheadings), Mrs. Slime attaches a tiny jewel-encrusted slime-catcher.

The McNastys knew that if they were going to swipe the treasure from under the children's noses they were going to have to act, and act fast. So they did. But you will have to read the next chapter to find out what it was they did, and I can tell you it is deeply, disgustingly and distressingly nasty and ghastly.

This page is not Chapter 4,
it is page 40. And along with page 41,
it features some outstandingly
helpful advice on how to read this book!

- WITH .

- IИ FЯOИT OF A MIЯЯOЯ
  BAƆKWAЯD.

- Very quickly.

- Wearing a blindfold.

- While picking that very tempting scab on
  your left knee.

- Under the covers with a flashlight
  that has the power of a million candles.

- While swimming — the pages are waterproof. (Sorry! If you just tried that you will know now that I was lying. Oh, and watch out — there's a shark behind you!)

- Openmouthed with admiration at what a staggeringly brilliant genius the author must be. (But do please be alert to the possibility that a bee or Quetzalcoatl might fly into your open mouth.)

- In Australia.

- Under the desk at school when you should be doing math problems.

Chapter 4

(I implore you to skip this chapter if you are of a nervous disposition or get hiccups very easily. Although if you do skip it, the rest of the story won't make any sense at all. This is what is known as "being on the horns of a dilemma.")

A horned dilemma

"Quick," said Captain Gruesome and Captain Grisly together as soon as they spied Tat and Hetty trying to lift the box out of the deep hole. "Launch the sharkmobile!"

"Aye, aye, Captains," sniffed Mrs. Slime, and she pressed a button on the great wheel of *The Rotten Apple* and the sharkmobile appeared on deck. The twins and Mrs. Slime climbed in and Mrs. Slime pressed another button. The sharkmobile plummeted downward like an out-of-control elevator, and exited *The Rotten Apple* through a hole in the bottom that had been helpfully nibbled by maggots. The sharkmobile shot green slime out of its periscope to seal up the hole again. The useful properties of Mrs. Slime's nasal secretions (that's snot to you and me) were the only reason that the McNastys didn't get rid of Mrs. Slime, despite her persistent and extremely irritating sniffling.

Just then Captain Gruesome McNasty realized that he had forgotten Pegleg Polly, whom he hated but took everywhere with him so he would look like a proper pirate, and Mrs. Slime realized that she had forgotten her box of tissues, so they had to go back, climb on deck and unlock the front door, which was very annoying and made the twins even more bad-tempered than usual. Then they headed toward the shore and whizzed up the beach, stopping very close to Hetty, Tat and Dog. They got out of the sharkmobile, tied it up behind some rowing boats and disguised themselves as trees.

Heh! Heh!
Can you spot two real treasure chests the McNastys will never find?

Hetty, Tat and Dog were so busy trying to open the box that they didn't immediately notice the three trees shuffling toward them. The trees were within a few yards of them when Tat turned around and saw them.

"Look," said Tat. "Walking trees."

"Don't be silly, Tat," said Hetty firmly. "Trees can't walk, and if they have started they should be stopped immediately because it is most untree-like behavior."

Dog looked interested. He trotted over to the trees, sniffed, cocked his leg by each of them and marked them.

"Sweaty socks!" said Captain Gruesome McNasty between clenched teeth as he felt a trickle of liquid down his trouser leg.

"Squeaky underpants!" muttered Captain Grisly McNasty as a warm puddle formed in his shoes.

The third tree sneezed.

"That tree has got a very nasty cold. I hope it's not catching," said Tat.

But Hetty wasn't listening because she was prying open the box. Tat and Dog moved closer. The trees shuffled nearer. There was a quick flash of gold before Hetty closed the box again. She grinned in delight.

"TREASURE!" shouted Tat.

At that moment Captain Gruesome McNasty shouted, "Mine!"

"Mine!" shouted Captain Grisly McNasty at the same time.

They both reached over to grab the box out of Hetty's arms. Hetty opened her mouth to say something, but just then Mrs. Slime sneezed.

A pile of snot hurtled straight toward her like a small green torpedo.

Hetty ducked and the twins bumped each other very hard on the head.

"Timber!" squawked Pegleg Polly as the twins toppled to the ground and their disguises fell away, exposing their horrible faces and their terrible teeth.

The children and Dog stared at the twins.

"Those aren't trees," said Tat.

"No," said Hetty. "I told you that trees can't walk." Then she added, because she knew everything, "They are the McNasty twins, the nastiest pirates ever to have sailed the seven seas. And that's their second mate, Mrs. Slime."

Mrs. Slime was trying to edge away unnoticed, which was not easy as she was leaving a slime trail like a giant slug.

Hetty considered the pirates' appalling teeth and shuddered. "Let that be a lesson to you," she said, pointing at the blackened stubs. "That is what comes of not brushing your teeth and never paying a visit to the dentist."

"Quick," said Tat. "Let's take the treasure box and hide it until my mom and dad get back."

"Can you think of somewhere safe?" asked Hetty.

"Thinking is such hard work," said Tat. Then he grinned. "I know where it will be safe. I know where the McNastys will never go." He whispered in Hetty's ear in case anyone was listening.

"Sometimes I think you are an unacknowledged genius, Tat," said Hetty. "We can use my wagon to move it there, then we can go back to my house for lunch. My mom is cooking spaghetti Bolognese. She's put extra carrots in especially for you, Tat."

A little while after the children had left, the McNasty twins awoke to find a party of Scouts burying them up to their necks in sand. They both had terrible headaches. Captain Gruesome's head felt as if it had been pureed in a cement mixer. Captain Grisly felt as if he had just spent four hours learning his eight times table.

This illustration
has been CENSORED
by the publisher as
unsuitable for
those of a nervous
disposition.

Pirates v.
Scouts.

Pirates: 20
Scouts: 0

After disposing of the Scouts, they staggered to the deep hole. They both leaned over and peered down, hoping that there might be another box of treasure that the children had overlooked. From far away at the very bottom of the hole, they could just make out some bright lights in the darkness, and when they looked more closely, they could see some upside-down people waving at them. The people looked very happy, and the McNasty  twins didn't like that one bit because they thought everyone should be miserable like them.

They thought they might cheer themselves up by getting Mrs. Slime to sneeze on the waving people, but just then four kangaroos bounced up

through the hole, bonked
and boxed the twins hard
on the nose and bottom and
hopped away.

"Sweaty socks!" said Captain
Gruesome, rubbing his nose. "I must
be seeing things after my bang on
the head."

He looked greedily around, but there was
no sign of Tat, Hetty and the box of treasure. "I
am going to find those nasty treasure-grabbing
children and sit on them until they are squashed as
flat as pancakes and tell me where they have taken
the treasure."

"Squeaky underpants!" said Captain Grisly,
rubbing his bottom. "I am going to catch those
horrid children who've stolen what is rightfully
mine and make them walk the plank into
shark-infested waters."

"Nasty boys!" squawked Pegleg Polly.

Captain Gruesome took a swipe at her but
missed.

Slime
Attack
Page

There were some fantastic words
and sentences on this page, including
*nincompoop, chocolate, discombobulated,
tender, dinosaurs, hot buttered toast,
unlimited candy, all homework banned, every
school closed for the next seven years, stay
up as late as you like, eating vegetables can
be harmful, are you quite sure you couldn't
manage a third hot chocolate and raspberry
ice-cream sundae?, fudge, funfair, quixotic*
and *smiles*. (*Smiles* is the longest word in the
English language as there is a mile between
the two *S*s.) Sadly, Mrs. Slime's slime has
engulfed them all, so you may not want
to handle this page too closely, and
if you do, please wash your
hands well afterward.

Beard bugs
escaping slime

help
us...

Chapter 5

Disguising themselves as long-lost relatives, the McNastys asked villagers where they might find two children and a cat that behaved like a dog. They were directed to Hetty's house. Still rubbing their sore heads, the McNastys arrived at Hetty's house just in time to see the children and Dog disappearing through the side door.

"Sweaty socks. They haven't got the box of treasure with them," said Captain Gruesome McNasty.

"Squeaky underpants! They must have hidden it in a secret place for safekeeping. We'll have to follow them and discover where they've put it," said Captain Grisly McNasty.

The twins sat down to keep watch on the children and eat their packed lunch of pickled onion and caterpillar sandwiches, which they thought were exceptionally delicious.

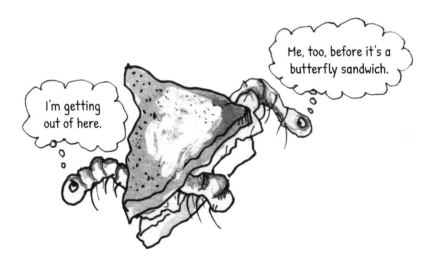

"What we need," said Captain Gruesome, "is a plan."

"Yes, a nasty, ghastly plan," said his brother.

It was not hard to come up with one because they were so very nasty and ghastly and because they had sent Mrs. Slime to the Captain Bluebeard Memorial Library to borrow a copy of *101 Ways to Dispose of Horrible, Horrendous and Hideous Children*.

"Aha, how admirably abominable," said Captain Gruesome, pointing to page 105, which had instructions on how to lure children into a Big, Scary, Very Dark, Dense Forest Where No One In Their Right Mind Would Want To Go.

"Indispensible to the childcare professional." Hairy Poppins

"I wish this book had been around in my day." King Herod

"A disgrace." Mrs. Trout, author of *Naming Your Children Responsibly*

"Look, how loathsomely lovely," said Captain Grisly, pointing to page 106 and a recipe for Truly Scrumptious, Perfectly Poisonous Jam Sandwich Flavored Fudge.

"Sweaty socks! We are brilliant brainiacs," said Captain Gruesome.

"Squeaky underpants! We are cunningly clever," said Captain Grisly. "We'll lure the children into the Big, Scary, Very Dark, Dense Forest Where No One In Their Right Mind Would Want To Go with the promise of fudge and make them confess where they have hidden the treasure and then steal it from them."

"Nasty boys!" squawked Pegleg Polly.

Captain Gruesome gave her a swipe with his hand and she fell all the way to page 86.

After lunch, the children set off toward the Little Snoring candy store. Hetty's mom had given them some money, and the children wanted to buy candy before heading back to the beach to dig for more treasure.

"Sweaty socks," growled Captain Gruesome, watching Hetty and Tat as they walked down the road with Dog trotting behind them. "It looks like those revolting children still haven't got the treasure box with them."

"Squeaky underpants," whined Captain Grisly. "Never mind, we'll have gruesome fun making them tell us where they have hidden it. Our cunning plan can't fail. We just have to get ahead of the children and put up our sign, which will lure them to their doom."

"We'll take a shortcut across Little Snoring's delightful junkyard," said Captain Gruesome, who always found the smell of junkyards strangely alluring.

The children passed several kangaroos grazing on the tulips in the front gardens, which was a bit puzzling as Hetty said she was quite certain that kangaroos lived in Australia and were not native to Little Snoring and she couldn't think how they had got there.

They arrived at the candy store, but there was a

big sign on the door saying:

"What a pity," said Hetty.

"It's very odd," said Tat. "The candy store is only ever closed on wet Wednesday afternoons in March and it's a Saturday in May today and hot and dry."

"Look!" said Hetty excitedly, and she pointed to a sign next to the candy store.

"Hetty," said Tat. "Don't you think this is highly suspicious? I wonder if it could be the McNastys trying to lure us into a trap."

"Oh, no," said Hetty, whose mouth was already watering at the prospect of free fudge. "The McNastys aren't smart enough to trap us."

"Are you quite sure, Hetty?" asked Tat.

"I am supremely confident," said Hetty, and Tat believed her because everyone knew that Hetty knew everything.

"It *is* very tempting," agreed Tat, who had never tasted jam sandwich flavored fudge and thought that he should, "but to get to it we'll have to walk through the Big, Scary, Very Dark, Dense Forest Where No One In Their Right Mind Would Want To Go."

"We would," agreed Hetty, who was discovering that the prospect of free fudge was making her feel unusually brave, "but we would be very careful, and what's a little fear, horror, dread, anxiety and trepidation when there is free fudge involved? And we can keep an eye out for more treasure."

"That's a great plan," said Tat. "Let's do it."

Chapter 6

Hetty and Tat set off through the Big, Scary, Very Dark, Dense Forest Where No One In Their Right Mind Would Want To Go.

The Big, Scary, Very Dark, Dense Forest Where No One In Their Right Mind Would Want To Go was exceptionally big, scary, dark and dense:

Tat was very brave and volunteered to go first because he had brought his flashlight with the power of a million candles with him, and Hetty knew that you should never eat the poisonous toadstools however pretty they looked and however many cute little elves were dancing around them.

They arrived at Ye Olde Fudge Shoppe where the McNasty twins and Mrs. Slime were disguised as kind, helpful fudge-shop keepers. The McNasty twins put on their ghastliest smiles and held out a big plate of Truly Scrumptious, Perfectly Poisonous Jam Sandwich Flavored Fudge.

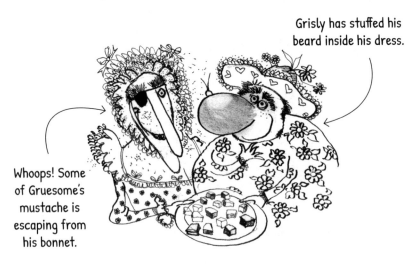

Grisly has stuffed his beard inside his dress.

Whoops! Some of Gruesome's mustache is escaping from his bonnet.

"Stop!" shouted Hetty, seeing through their disguises, but she was too late: Tat and Dog had already gobbled down several pieces each.

"Aha!" said the McNasty twins, tearing off their disguises. "Got you, you rotten-toothed children!"

They turned to Hetty.

"I'm delighted to inform you," said Captain Gruesome, "that the nasty boy and nasty cat have just been poisoned by our Truly Scrumptious, Perfectly Poisonous Jam Sandwich Flavored Fudge. And if you don't tell us where you've hidden the treasure that you found this morning, we won't give them the antidote."

"Actually," Captain Grisly muttered, "we don't know the antidote."

Hetty frowned. "If you don't have the antidote," she said, "there is no logical reason why

I should tell you where the treasure is. Telling you won't save Tat and Dog."

"You bumbling, bimbling idiot!" roared Captain Gruesome to his brother. "You've ruined my dastardly plan!"

"Excuse me, but you've ruined my life, which, although it hasn't been going too well recently, is the only one I have," whispered Tat quietly but very bravely.

"Yes," said Captain Grisly, "but let's look on the bright side. At least we've rid the world of one more horrible, hideous child and a naughty, nasty cat that behaves like a dog."

"Show me the recipe," demanded Hetty.

Captain Gruesome grinned wickedly as he watched Hetty read the list of ingredients, which looked like this:

TRULY SCRUMPTIOUS, PERFECTLY POISONOUS JAM SANDWICH FLAVORED FUDGE *

1. One tail of dead rat
2. The fifth toe of a three-toed sloth
3. One teaspoon Wombat Dung
4. The spit of two pink flamingos
5. One UNWASHED GYM UNIFORM (including smelly socks that has been left in the gym bag over the summer holidays)
6. One liter of cold custard (skin on)
7. Two tablespoons of rhino toe-clippings
8. A sprinkling of diced cockroach
9. Two-week-old hair from the shower drain
10. Four pots of BEST strawberry jam
11. One sliced loaf (the older and moldier the better)

N.B. Resist the understandable desire to add two pints of slime & up the disturbing realism the recipe involves!!!!

* Serves 2 Kids + 1 Cat

Hetty scanned the ingredients. She turned green and then she turned white.

"It really is poisonously poisonous, isn't it?" said Captain Grisly happily.

"Alas, yes," whispered Hetty. "All is lost!" A tear rolled down her cheek.

"Should Dog and I say goodbye, Hetty?" asked Tat bravely.

"Yes," said Hetty tearfully.

"Goodbye," said Tat.

"Meow," meowed Dog.

He rolled over on his side and wagged his tail feebly.

"The poison is working even quicker than I'd hoped," said Captain Grisly.

"That's because I made it even more poisonous!" said Captain Gruesome triumphantly. "I put in two extra ingredients."

"What did you add?" asked Hetty urgently.

"Two pints of green slime and a pig's ear."

"Two pints of green slime and a pig's ear?" said Hetty. She smiled and picked up one of the pieces of fudge and ate it.

"Mmm … Truly scrumptious."

"Hetty, what on earth are you doing?" cried Tat. "You'll be poisoned, too."

"No, I won't," said Hetty calmly. "I came across this same recipe in a book when I was doing my Super Star–winning school project on Lives of the Great Poisoners (Regretful and Reformed) and it was quite clear that the recipe is not effective if you add two pints of slime and a pig's ear. It stops all the other ingredients from working."

Captain Gruesome seized the recipe book. Sure enough, at the very bottom of the recipe was a footnote in tiny writing that declared that anyone following the recipe must:

NB. **Resist** the understandable desire to add two pints of slime & a pig's ear. This will render the recipe harmless !!!!

The McNasty twins roared with rage like rampaging rhinoceroses and ran off. (Actually, they slunk off quietly, furious that their dastardly plan had entirely failed to work, but I enjoyed writing a sentence with so many *R*s in it and it's fun to roll your *R*s when you are reading out loud.)

Mrs. Slime sneezed. "ACHOO!"

Misery made her sneezes even more explosive than usual. She liked Tat and Hetty far more than she liked the McNastys, who had confiscated her box of tissues when a sneezing attack made her late back from the library. Green slime poured out of her nose like a fast-flowing river.

Hetty shuddered and handed Mrs. Slime her only clean tissue.

"Thank you, you're too kind," said Mrs. Slime with a grateful sniffle, and she reluctantly set off in the direction taken by the McNastys, leaving a trail of slime behind her. "I'll give the tissue back to you when I see you next," she called.

"That really won't be necessary," said Hetty hurriedly. "Please keep it."

"I think Mrs. Slime is more sad than bad," said Tat thoughtfully.

"You're right, Tat. There's nothing about that woman that a little kindness and a lifetime supply of tissues wouldn't cure. Here," said Hetty, "have another piece of fudge. It is truly scrumptious as long as you don't think too hard about what's in it."

"Oh, Hetty," said Tat with a mixture of relief and admiration. "Dog and I are lucky that you know everything."

Strictly, this was not true, because Hetty had not known that Ye Olde Fudge Shoppe was a nasty trick thought up by the McNastys. In fact, there were quite a lot of other things that Hetty did not know: she did not know where all the lost teddy bears in the world go, or why there is always fluff in your belly button or whether the fridge light stays on even when you shut the door, or how much wood the woodchuck would chuck if the woodchuck could chuck wood.

Chapter 7

Hetty, Tat and Dog walked back through the Big, Scary, Very Dark, Dense Forest Where No One In Their Right Mind Would Want To Go. They thought it was even bigger, scarier, darker and nastier, and they were right because it now had the McNasty twins in it who made everything bigger, scarier, darker and nastier as well as stenchier, smellier and stinkier.

"Well, that was a lucky escape," said Tat, as Dog bounded through the forest in front of the children.

"I don't think luck has anything to do with it," said Hetty, a little sniffily. Hetty was feeling rather tired and you shouldn't underestimate how difficult it is to walk any distance in odd shoes. But she perked up when she thought of the treasure box. She was looking forward to examining its wondrous contents carefully.

Still, Hetty was feeling a little embarrassed that Tat had been the one who had been suspicious about the fudge shop and she had fallen for the McNastys' ruse. She felt guilty that Tat and Dog had almost been poisoned and it was making her unusually quiet.

"Hetty," said Tat. "You really were very clever to spot the flaw in the jam sandwich fudge recipe."

"And you were very clever and very brave, Tat," said Hetty generously, "and often it's harder to be brave than clever." And she meant it.

Cleverness came easily to Hetty, but she found it much harder to be brave like Tat. Then she added, "The McNasty twins are neither brave nor clever but they are not quite as stupid as I thought. I'm furious that I let us fall for their trick. It just goes to show that you should never underestimate the enemy."

"No," said Tat thoughtfully, "but if they can lay traps for us, we can lay traps for them, too. We need to teach them a lesson or they will keep trying to snatch our treasure box."

"Do you have a plan, Tat?"

"I do," said Tat, and he began to outline it.

A look of admiration flashed across Hetty's eyes. "You deserve a Super Star, Tat," she said. "Miss Green is very silly not to recognize that people can be clever in many different ways."

The McNastys were sitting by a bog.

"What we need," said Captain Grisly, "is a scoundrelly plan that is more rotten than a crate of maggoty fish."

Captain Gruesome scratched his mustache, and forty-four fleas and two nits took the opportunity to make their escape.

"We must find the children, kidnap them and make them walk the plank unless they tell us what they've done with the treasure. This time nothing must go wrong." He grinned nastily. "The lost treasure of Little Snoring will soon be all mine."

"And mine," said Captain Grisly and he whacked his brother, who walloped him back, and they whacked and walloped each other so hard that they fell into the foul-smelling bog. They might have been sucked into its depths and drowned if Mrs. Slime hadn't arrived in the nick of time and pulled them both out.

The McNastys didn't even say thank you. In fact, they were so annoyed that Mrs. Slime had taken so long to find them that they pushed her into the oozing bog and set off in pursuit of the children, ignoring all her pleas for help.

Luckily for Mrs. Slime a truly explosive sneeze soon propelled her to the edge and she was able to crawl out of the bog unaided, although with several leeches stuck to her face.

The twins walked round and round the forest for some time and they might still be there if they hadn't accidentally stumbled across a path.

They looked up the path and they looked down the path but they didn't know which way the children had gone.

Then Captain Grisly suddenly spied a jam sandwich. They walked a little farther and they came across a splotch of jam and then another sandwich. The brothers grinned wickedly at each other. Those foolish children obviously didn't realize that they were leaving a jam sandwich trail behind them. All the McNastys had to do was to follow the trail and they would find the children and frighten them so badly that they would immediately confess where they had hidden the golden treasure that the McNastys had glimpsed in the box.

Chapter 8

Xtra Big Booger-Wrappers (for HUGE honkers)

Hetty and Tat were hiding in the bushes close to the shore. They had stopped off at the village store and used their candy money to buy an extra-large box of tissues, a bottle of cold medicine, some big sheets of cardboard and a black felt-tip pen. They were now within sight of the

McNastys' sharkmobile, which was still tied up close to several rowing boats.

"I don't know," said Hetty, which was the first time those three words had ever crossed her lips, "perhaps we should just give the McNastys the treasure we found. Then maybe they will leave us alone and sail away and never come back to Little Snoring."

"No," said Tat fiercely. "We can't do that. We put all the work into finding that treasure. Why should we be bullied into handing it over to the greedy McNastys? Besides, maybe my plan will work. If we can keep them on *The Rotten Apple* for the rest of today and tonight, my parents and Tallulah will be back early tomorrow morning and we can give them the treasure. We may even have found some more by then."

Hetty squeezed his hand, but she was still worried.

"Tat, it's a brilliant, brainiac idea to lure the McNastys back to the sea with a jam trail, but what you are proposing is dangerous, too. If they capture you, they will make you walk the plank."

"They won't capture me," said Tat, "because although I'm not very good at math, I can row very fast."

"Let Dog and me come with you," pleaded Hetty.

"You'll only slow me down," said Tat, and Hetty knew that he was right.

She watched as he untied a rowing boat, pushed it out to sea and jumped in.

"Good luck, Tat."

"Thanks, Hetty, I'm going to need it."

Tat rowed a little bit away from the shore and then stopped.

Hetty sat down in the bushes and waited.

After a few minutes she heard a sneeze. She raised her head cautiously above the bush.

Mrs. Slime was standing on the beach. There was no sign of the McNastys.

"Mrs. Slime," hissed Hetty.

Mrs. Slime turned around and sneezed. Hetty ducked just in time.

"Mrs. Slime," said Hetty urgently, "I'd like to make you an offer that you can't possibly refuse."

The McNastys were extremely grumpy. They had followed the jam sandwich trail all through the Big, Scary, Very Dark, Dense Forest Where No One In Their Right Mind Would Want To Go. Their feet were covered in jam and they stuck to the path with every step and they kept attracting the unwanted attention of swarms of angry wasps. They were also being pestered by kangaroos who wanted to lick the jam off their feet.

When the McNastys demanded payment in return for the jam, the kangaroos boxed their ears. As a result the McNastys had made very slow progress.

But eventually they stumbled out of the forest and through the village, and followed the trail right to the very edge of the sea.

They looked up and across the water. Between them and *The Rotten Apple* was a rowing boat, and sitting in the rowing boat was Tat.

He grinned and waved at them, then stood up very carefully. He was holding several sheets of

cardboard. He held up the first sheet. On it was
written in big black letters:

He dropped the first sheet and underneath was
a second sheet that declared:

The McNastys growled at him like angry
Rottweilers and shook their fists.

Tat grinned and produced a third sheet.

The McNastys yelped furiously and shook their fists again.

Tat held up a fourth sheet.

Tat dropped that sheet to reveal a fifth and final message.

CATCH ME
IF YOU
CAN!

With that, Tat sat down in the boat and began rowing as fast as he could toward *The Rotten Apple*. The McNastys screeched with horror and fury at the thought of losing all their treasure. They ran toward the sharkmobile. But then they remembered that Mrs. Slime had the ignition key in her pocket.

"Mrs. Slime! Mrs. Slime!" they cried. But there was no answer. They watched, horrified, as Tat's dinghy moved closer and closer to their unoccupied ship, which was stuffed full of treasure.

"Sweaty socks!" said Captain Gruesome. "That maggoty boy is going to board our ship and steal our treasure!" Then a look of relief passed across his face. "But he won't get in. The front door is locked."

"Ooops!" said Captain Grisly. "I've just remembered. I forgot to lock it."

The twins stared at each other, aghast. Then they raced for one of the rowing boats and started rowing after Tat as fast as they could, which was not very fast at all because they kept fighting.

Behind the bushes, Mrs. Slime took a big swig of cold medicine and accepted another tissue from Hetty. Hetty smiled at her, and Mrs. Slime smiled back. She hadn't had a close friend since she had caught her cold, which was thirty-eight years ago. She was certain that Hetty and Tat would be true friends. True friends never complain about sniffling, even though it is a most irritating habit.

This is where poor Pegleg fell from page 57.

DISCLAIMER

The author takes no responsibility whatsoever for readers who decide to read the next chapter despite this warning because you are probably the sort of person who sees signs saying DO NOT WALK ON THE GRASS and walks on it anyway, and then are very indignant when the grass turns out not to be grass but 242 hungry crocodiles. So don't say you haven't been WARNED.

Twice.

(Sadly there is no Chapter 9
because seven ate nine.)

Chapter 10

Tat rowed as hard as he could. He reached *The Rotten Apple*, climbed up the rope ladder and clambered onto the deck. The McNastys were still a long way away from the ship.

Tat ran along the deck, through the unlocked front door, which was swinging wide open, and into the McNastys' bedroom. He was shocked to see that Captain Grisly's teddy bear was perched perilously on a plank above a massive tank of hungry piranhas. He imagined Grisly making his poor teddy walk the plank.

Tat pressed a slightly jammy finger against the outside of the glass tank and was horrified when the fish all swam toward it, their razor teeth snapping. Tat jumped back, rescued the teddy bear and put him safely on the bed.

He looked around. In the corner of the
bedroom was a large treasure chest. It was full of
diamonds and rubies, silver goblets and gold bars.
Tat looked longingly at the stolen treasure.

One little diamond or ruby was all his family
needed. It was so tempting. He reached out a hand
toward a gold bar, and then snatched it back again.
If he took something, it would be stealing. He
would be as bad as the McNastys. Sadly, he closed
the treasure box. In any case, treasure wasn't what
he had come for — he just wanted the McNastys
to think that.

He took a note out of his pocket and placed it artfully in the middle of the floor so it looked as if it had just been accidentally dropped there. Then he ran back onto the deck.

The McNastys were still huffing and puffing their way toward *The Rotten Apple*. Tat ran to the other side of the deck and climbed nimbly down the rope ladder. He waited until he heard the McNastys begin to climb the rope ladder on the other side of the ship and then he dived into the sea, swam under *The Rotten Apple* and set off, swimming underwater toward the shore.

The McNastys rushed into their bedroom. The first thing they checked was their treasure chest. They were puzzled. Their treasure was all accounted for and there was no sign of the nasty boy. They rushed out onto the deck to find him but it was empty. They looked over the deck and toward the shore but there was no sign of him. They searched the entire ship, and even looked in the boiler room, which was a bit scary because it was full of bats and rats. Captain Gruesome made Captain Grisly look under his bed where the dust was almost two inches high and a family of giant cockroaches was moving out. One of the cockroaches bit Captain Grisly on the nose.

The McNastys were foxed and flummoxed. They were relieved that all their treasure was safe but where could Tat have possibly gone? He was nowhere to be found on *The Rotten Apple* and yet his dinghy was still tied up by the rope ladder. He seemed to have disappeared into thin air. It never occurred to them that Tat was a champion swimmer and had swum all the way back to shore, because the McNastys didn't know how to swim. They had been expelled from Pirate School before they had even had the chance to get their ten-meter breaststroke swimming certificate.

They sat down on their bedroom floor by the big tank of piranhas to have a good think, which hurt quite a lot. Captain Grisly suddenly noticed that his teddy was no longer perched on the plank above the fish tank where he had left him. He stood up and examined the tank. He spotted the fingerprint of jam on the side.

"Squeaky underpants! I know what has happened to that nasty boy. He must have fallen in the tank. My pretty, precious piranhas have had a good meal. They have gobbled every last gobbet of him. That's why we can find no trace of him."

The McNastys laughed so nastily that even the blue in the sky momentarily turned black.

At that moment they both spied the crumpled piece of paper on the floor. They grabbed for it at the same time, and as neither of them would let go, it tore into several bits. Eventually they pieced it together again and began to read. The note had a large, sticky jam stain in a corner, but the McNastys could read the part of the message that interested them.

OFFICIAL

Expect ship bearing precious cargo to arrive
at Little Snoring tonight.

The McNastys smiled toothily. They knew
precious cargo was code for TREASURE.

"Sweaty socks! It's turning into a wickedly
wonderful day for gruesomeness. The note
must have fallen out of that boy's pocket when
he tumbled into the fish tank," said Captain
Gruesome.

"Squeaky underpants! It's becoming the most
dastardly delightful day for grisliness," agreed his
brother.

"We've rid the world of a maggoty child, and
now all we have to do is sit here on our ship and
lure the boat that comes tonight onto the Jaws so
we can steal its precious cargo of treasure."

"What about the Little Snoring treasure?" asked Captain Grisly.

"It can wait. It will still be there for us to steal tomorrow. One treasure in a McNasty hand is worth two in the bush."

Chapter 11

T at looked out his bedroom window and across the sea. It was almost midnight and it was a dark and cheerless night. Even the moon was sulking miserably behind a cloud and the moonbeams were all shivering and huddling together like penguins trying to keep warm.

After checking his teeth thoroughly and

making him do a second brush of them, Aunt Tessie had told Tat to go to bed. But Tat couldn't sleep. He was too excited. He couldn't wait to show his mom and dad the treasure when they rowed home tomorrow.

He hadn't been able to eat his dinner either, even though Aunt Tessie had made him triple helpings of jam sandwiches. (Aunt Tessie didn't believe in giving children jam sandwiches for their dinner because jam is very bad for teeth, but she had made an exception because she thought Tat needed cheering up.) Tat had stuffed the sandwiches in his dressing gown pocket in case he felt peckish later. Tat had once eaten seventeen jam sandwiches — it had made him burp seventy-two times, which he thought might be a world record, and he didn't want to be burping all night.

Dog suddenly gave a loud mew and sat up, very alert. There was a tapping on the window. Tat leaped out of bed. On the ledge there was a bedraggled carrier seagull. It was carrying a note in its mouth. Tat quickly unfurled the paper.

He recognized the writing immediately.

Change of plan.
We are coming back tonight.
Tell Aunt Tessie.

Love, Dad

Tat gasped. His mom, dad and Tallulah
were rowing back to the island tonight! What if
the McNastys mistook them for the boat with
precious cargo?

He had eaten an extra carrot that morning and
his eyesight was better than ever. In the distance,
far away on the horizon, he was certain he could
see a pinprick of light bobbing about. He knew
it must be his family in their sturdy little rowing
boat.

Tat felt sick. He had thought he was being so
clever by making the McNastys wait all night for

a boat that would never come, but now one was! And it had the most valuable cargo in the world in it: his family. His actions had put his family in danger. He was wondering what he should do when he saw another light, much nearer and brighter. It began to blink at regular intervals, like the beam from a lighthouse.

Tat frowned. He knew that there shouldn't be a light coming from that location because there was nothing there. Nothing, that is, except the sandbanks and the Jaws upon which many a ship and boat had been wrecked before the Little Snoring lighthouse had been built. The lighthouse! The cogs in Tat's brain began to whirr and click like a cuckoo clock on the fritz.

Tat ran to the back of the house, which looked up the cliffs to where the lighthouse was perched. It was in complete darkness.

Tat thought hard. He may not be very good at Miss Green's kind of math but he knew for certain that two McNastys plus one darkened lighthouse and one light blinking by the Jaws didn't make four, it made an epic disaster of infinite proportions for the Trout family. The McNastys were trying to lure his family onto the rocks. He had to save his parents and Tallulah!

His heart began to thump louder than the music at the annual Little Snoring junior fancy dress disco.

Tat raced down the stairs. Aunt Tessie was snoring quietly in her armchair. She had fallen asleep over her 443 516–piece jigsaw puzzle that she had bought at the same store where she had bought Tat's flashlight with the power of a million candles. Tat didn't stop to wake her up. He opened the front door and with Dog at his side he began running for the beach.

When he was down on the sand, his superior eyesight meant that despite the darkness of the night he could see *The Rotten Apple* moored at a spot just this side of the Jaws so it was completely obscured from the approaching boat. He looked up at *The Rotten Apple*'s mast. Flying from the top was the skull and crossbones. The terrible sound of the McNastys' laughter could just be heard carried upon the wind as, at regular intervals, they shone a flashlight out to sea.

Tat didn't hesitate. He had to stop the McNastys.

"Hetty, wake Hetty," he told Dog, who meowed loudly and wagged his tail to show he understood.

Tat ran over to one of the little rowing boats, pushed it into the water and started rowing as fast as he could toward *The Rotten Apple*.

Tat rowed as hard and as silently as possible, and tried to block out the terrible sound of the McNastys' laughter, which was like a room full of balloons being rubbed together. He rowed alongside *The Rotten Apple*, lined his boat up with the rope ladder and tied it to the bottom rung alongside the two other rowing boats that had been left there.

Then he began to climb up the side of *The Rotten Apple*, leaning back slightly to try and avoid the worms coming out of the ship's rotten wooden planks that tried to lick his face as he passed. Tat climbed higher and higher until he reached the handrail that ran around the top of the deck. Very carefully, he peered over the top …

Chapter 12

Hetty woke up with a jump to the sound of meowing, which is much, much nicer than waking up to the sound of a screeching alarm clock. She looked around. It was still very dark. It was obviously far too early to get up and start trying to do six impossible things before breakfast, which, to tell the truth, she was beginning to find quite exhausting. She thought that maybe she should just try to do six impossible things before breakfast on Monday, Wednesday and Friday and skip breakfast on the other days.

She lay in bed for a moment, but the meowing just got louder, and as she lay there she became aware of an intermittent beam of light outside her bedroom window. Hetty's sleepy brain, which had not quite woken up yet and really wanted to carry on dreaming, tried to make her roll over and snuggle under the duvet. But Hetty forced it to think.

Suddenly she leaped out of bed, grabbed her glasses and ran over to the window. Hetty found it utterly impossible to eat six carrots before breakfast however hard she tried, but at that moment the moon briefly appeared from behind a cloud and she could see the hulk of *The Rotten Apple* moored by the Jaws.

She could see that the ship was also the source of the blinking light and she knew at once that the Ghastly McNastys were trying to lure some poor sailors out on this filthy night toward the treacherous rocks.

Hetty knew that the McNastys were wasting their time. There was no boat with precious cargo. The note that Tat had left on *The Rotten Apple* for the McNastys to find was an old one dating from the time when Tat's dad had been the lighthouse keeper. Clever Tat was just using it as a way to keep the McNastys on their ship until his parents and sister returned and he could give them the treasure that he and Hetty had dug up on the beach. There was no need to worry.

She looked across the sea, which was growing wilder as the wind began to shriek. It was as if it had suddenly glimpsed something very, very frightening.

At that moment, Hetty spotted the little rowing boat leaving the harbor of Little Snoring and setting out on the frothing sea toward *The Rotten Apple*.

Dog was pointing his paw toward it and mewing loudly, and Hetty was certain that Tat must be in that little boat.

Hetty's stomach sank to her toes, which made a terrible clanging noise that echoed around her bedroom and made her worry that it might wake up her parents. After she picked her stomach up and put it back where it belonged, she put on her dressing gown, ran downstairs and opened the front door. Dog tried to jump up and lick her face, then he bounded ahead of her as they both ran down to the beach and toward the sea.

Right at the water's edge lay a jam sandwich, immediately confirming to Hetty that it was Tat in the rowing boat. But why was he going back to

The Rotten Apple? She knew that Tat must have a very good reason to do something so dangerous.

Then she realized that the lighthouse was in darkness. Being the kind of girl she was, Hetty put two and two together and came up with 125 and a half. She guessed that the McNastys must have stopped it working.

She turned back to *The Rotten Apple* and what she saw was so frightful that I can hardly bear to write the words, but I will be very brave, maybe even braver than a dormouse or a llama, and try.

What she saw was Tat climbing the rope ladder up the side of *The Rotten Apple*. She saw him pop his head cautiously over the edge of the handrail and then she saw two pairs of hairy arms reach out, grab him hard and lift him over.

The McNasty twins had captured Tat!

For the first time in her life, Hetty didn't know what to do, but what she did know was that she must save Tat before the McNasty twins made him walk the plank or keelhauled him. Tat had told Hetty about the poor teddy who was perched perilously on a plank above a tank full of piranhas, and she feared for his life. Anyone wicked enough to think of feeding their teddy bear to piranha fish would have no qualms about making a small boy walk the plank.

Hetty shivered. She knew she was going to have to do something very brave, something so brave that it would make doing six impossible things before breakfast seem easy peasy.

She heard a gentle sneeze behind her.

"I think," said Mrs. Slime, "that it's time for me to help you in return for your kindness in alleviating the symptoms of my cold."

Chapter 13

(Unlucky for some)

The McNastys were confused, and being confused always made them as angry as terrapins.

Their plan, to lure onto the rocks the ship carrying precious cargo detailed in the note they had found on their bedroom floor, had been going rather well. They had successfully stopped the beam of the lighthouse by dropping a very large blanket over it from a helicopter, which had cost half their treasure to hire. But it was worth it to get their nasty hands on more treasure. The prize had been in sight.

They had both glimpsed the lamp from a rowing boat as it set off just after 11:00 p.m. from the mainland and headed toward the island and the harbor of Little Snoring. It did seem to be quite a small boat to be carrying such a huge precious cargo, but they guessed that what was on board was so priceless that the owners didn't want to draw attention to it. They had used their flashlight to trick the boat into thinking it was heading for the harbor when in fact it was on a direct course for the sandbanks and the Jaws. The treasure would soon be theirs.

They were just about to start celebrating when they heard a noise and spied Tat climbing over the handrail on deck.

For a moment they were both frightened because they thought that Tat had been eaten by piranhas and that his ghost had come back to haunt them. But then they realized that he was a real flesh and blood boy because he was shouting "Stop!" and gabbling on about the fact that the rowing boat didn't contain any treasure, only the Trout family.

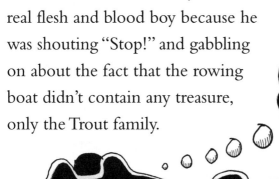

"Dastardly boy! You're trying to trick us and save the boat and keep its precious cargo out of our hands," said the twins angrily.

"No," said Tat desperately. "I'm not. There is no precious cargo. I dropped the note to trick you. If you look very carefully under the jam splotch, you'll see that the message dates from years ago."

The twins shone their flashlight on the note and saw that Tat was telling the truth.

The McNastys stamped their feet so hard that their left legs went straight through the rotten planks on deck.

They caught Tat in a net and squirted him with slime. Then the McNasty twins shone their flashlight with the power of five million candles in Tat's eyes.

It was rather painful, but it hurt less because Tat very cleverly realized that if the McNastys were shining their flashlight into his eyes they couldn't be using it to pretend to be the Little Snoring lighthouse and trick his mom and dad into rowing onto the Jaws. He glanced out toward

114

the sea and blinked to restore his vision. Without a light to guide it, the little boat had stopped moving. Tat heaved a sigh of relief.

He glanced the other way, and he spied another boat leaving Little Snoring and heading toward them. He hoped that Hetty was in the boat and that help was on its way. All he had to do was stall for time.

"We want to know exactly what's going on!" roared Captain Gruesome.

"We need information and we need it quickly," bawled Captain Grisly.

"Yes," said Captain Gruesome, "tell us EVERYTHING, absolutely EVERYTHING you know."

Tat stared at them. "Do you mean every single thing?"

"Yes!" roared Captain Grisly.

"Okay," said Tat with a smile. "If you're quite sure it will be of help." He took a deep breath.

Two and two is four.
i before *e* except after *c*.
Henry the Eighth had six wives.
You should never mess with badgers.
Raccoons can't swim. Nobody has ever
seen an ostrich with its head buried
in the sand. Leonardo da Vinci could
draw with his left hand while writing
with his right hand. Hair still grows
after you die. You should wash
your hands before eating.

The largest organ in your body is your skin. Hetty knows everything. Turtles can breathe through their bottoms. An abominable snowman and a yeti are the same thing but probably don't exist at all. If you swallow an apple core a tree might grow inside you. More people die from coconuts falling on their heads than by being eaten by sharks. You should never walk through the Big, Scary, Very Dark, Dense Forest Where No One In Their Right Mind Would Want To Go even if there is an offer of free fudge at the other end. The capital of Burkina Faso is Ouagadougou. Eating too many carrots turns you orange. Babies are often quite annoying but seldom get rabies. It is impossible to dig to Australia. *Difficulty* is very difficult to spell, particularly if you are feeling flustered and then *particularly* is quite hard, too.

Beware of sneezing trees. Peanut butter sandwiches are nice but jam sandwiches are better. Drinking seawater sends you mad. If you are hit by an avalanche you should try to swim out of it with breaststroke movements. The Nile is the world's longest river. Hetty is my best friend. Crocodiles don't make good pets ...

Tat was running out of breath, but it didn't matter because Captain Gruesome had fallen asleep and Captain Grisly was trying to spell *difficulty* and *particularly*. Tat stopped speaking and Captain Gruesome woke up with a jump.

"Clearly this nasty, nauseous, noxious ninny knows nothing of use. He is a complete waste of space," he said.

"Oh," said Tat indignantly, "I thought I told you quite a lot and I haven't even started yet on all the things Hetty has taught me."

"Silence," said Captain Grisly McNasty. "You will be dealt with. Gruesome, fetch the plank and some meat to attract the sharks."

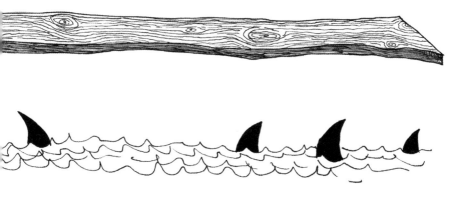

Chapter 14

Hetty rowed furiously toward *The Rotten Apple* with Dog in tow. She had discovered that rowing was much harder than it looked (which made her admire Tat a great deal more). The boat was quite heavy because, as they pushed off from the shore, several kangaroos had leaped on board.

Pegleg Polly is making her way through the story.

The McNasty twins didn't see Hetty's boat coming because Captain Gruesome was setting up the plank on the far side of the ship and Captain Grisly was dropping chunks of bloody raw meat into the sea to attract as many sharks as possible.

As soon as everything was ready, the McNastys shone the flashlight in Tat's eyes again.

"You are going to die so you might as well tell us where you've hidden the treasure. It's the least you can do for wasting our time," said Captain Gruesome.

Tat said nothing. He would never tell.

"Make him walk the plank!" cried Captain Grisly, before Tat had a chance to reply.

So they tied Tat's hands behind him and prodded him with a broom handle toward the end of the plank. Tat could hear the snapping of sharks' teeth.

Suddenly a big beam of light swept across the sea. It was such a welcome sight that it quite took Tat's mind off the prospect of imminent death.

The lighthouse was working again! In the distance, Tat saw the rowing boat, containing his family, begin to move again. It changed course and began heading straight for the safe haven of the harbor mouth. Tat was staring death straight in the face but he gave a loud laugh of happiness. His family was safe. He would die happy.

Infuriated, the McNastys prodded him harder toward the end of the plank. Then, with a nasty cackle, they gave him one last hard push and he disappeared over the edge. They stood waiting for the splash and the crunch of sharks' teeth against the small boy. But no splash or crunch came.

"Sweaty socks! A shark must have swallowed that nasty boy whole!"

"Squeaky underpants! It will give the shark the most terrible indigestion!"

But Tat had not been swallowed by a shark at all. He had jumped straight into Hetty's boat, which she had cleverly rowed around the side of *The Rotten Apple* so it was directly below the plank. Hetty untied Tat's hands and gave him a wet tissue to wipe away the slime. Then Tat began rowing them back to shore but not before the kangaroos had leaped onto the deck of *The Rotten Apple* and started whacking and walloping the McNasty twins on their noses and behinds.

"Sweaty socks! Set sail at once!" shouted Captain Gruesome to Mrs. Slime. But Mrs. Slime was not there. She was sitting by the lighthouse, blowing her nose very loudly into the blanket, which she had pulled down. It was the biggest handkerchief she had ever seen, and Hetty had promised that if she could get it down from the lighthouse, she could keep it.

Despite being boxed continuously by the kangaroos, the McNasty twins finally got *The Rotten Apple* underway and it sailed farther out into the open sea. But they didn't get very far.

Pegleg Polly, who had been slowly
climbing up from page 86, where
she had been swiped by Captain
Gruesome, got to page 120 and found
herself right in the thick of the story.
Eager to get her revenge, she flew
down into the bowels of the ship and pulled
out Mrs. Slime's snot plug with her beak. It came
out with a satisfying pop. It took a few minutes for
The Rotten Apple to start to take on water.

But when it did there was an enormous GLUG.

And then there was a huge GURGLE.

Then there were lots of little gurgles.

And then *The Rotten Apple* began to sink.

The kangaroos and various rats and bats jumped
overboard and swam or flew back to shore.

The Rotten Apple was sinking fast. Captain
Gruesome and Captain Grisly turned red,
then purple with rage and then green and
white with fear.

"Sweaty socks! We are staring catastrophe in the face!" Actually catastrophe doesn't have a face, but this is what it would look like if it did:

"Squeaky underpants! This is a disaster!"
Captain Grisly had never spoken a truer word.
(Or six words in this case.)

When the water came up
to their knees, the McNasty
twins jumped overboard but
they didn't look before they
leaped and they jumped straight
into the mouth of an enormous whale
— the very same one that they had bumped on
the nose on the way to Little Snoring. The whale
had followed them and had been lying in wait for
them so she could teach them a few manners.

Just then *The Rotten Apple* disappeared with a
sound that was like something too big going down
the bath drain.

The whale gave an enormous burp and from somewhere in its stomach could be heard the words, *Sweaty socks* and *Squeaky underpants*. The whale swam very fast, far out into the ocean, to join the rest of her family.

Tat rowed back to shore with Hetty and Dog. The sky was taking on the rosy hue of dawn. He rowed hard toward the harbor mouth and arrived there just at the same time as his parents' boat.

"Why did you come back early?" he asked when they were all standing on the seashore together.

"Ah," said his dad. "All the jewelers were closed. They'd been offered a last-minute bargain weekend trip to Ouagadougou."

"So you couldn't sell the wedding ring?"

"No," said Tat's mom, "but actually I'm pleased. Some things are worth more than money."

"But we did buy jam donuts," piped up Tallulah.

"Yes," said Tat's dad. "We spent the last of our money on them."

"Jam makes everything seem better," said Hetty brightly.

"It does." Tat's mom smiled. "And something will turn up."

"Actually," said Tat, "it already has."

They all started to walk toward the village.

"By the way, Tat," said Tat's dad. "Was that the Ghastly McNastys' ship I saw sinking?"

Tat nodded.

"I hope they haven't been bothering you."

Tat grinned at Hetty. "Nothing we couldn't handle," he said. "We'll tell you all about it over jam donuts."

Later that day, everyone in the village of Little Snoring gathered on the beach. Tat and Hetty wheeled down the wagon carrying the big wooden box, which they'd draped in an old blue velvet curtain covered with silver stars that had been used in the village pantomime. The school band played a fanfare, and everybody watched with mounting excitement as Tat removed the curtain with a flourish. He grinned at Hetty, and together they slowly raised the lid of the box. There was a flash of gold and a loud gasp from the crowd, followed by a tiny silence, and then everyone began cheering wildly and clapping Tat and Hetty on the back. The box was full of precious TREASURE. It was all the lost shoes that had gone missing from the houses in Little Snoring over the last few months.

Hetty's mom's missing gold sandal glinted right at the top. She reached for it with an enormous smile on her face, and soon the rest of the delighted villagers were reclaiming their lost shoes. For the first time in months some people in the village had two shoes that matched, and it made them want to dance.

They happily handed over the reward money to Hetty and Tat, but Hetty said that it all belonged to Tat because if it hadn't been for him being so brave and clever, then nobody would have got their shoes back.

"So where did you hide the box that the

McNastys would never think of looking?" asked Tat's dad after they had told everyone about their adventures and how the McNastys had tried to snaffle the box, believing it was stuffed full of jewels and gold bars.

"We took it to Aunt Tessie's dental office," said Tat. "After we'd seen the McNastys' teeth, we knew they'd never go there."

"Actually," said Hetty, who was staring hard at Miss Green, "it was all Tat's brilliant idea."

Miss Green had the grace to look a little embarrassed. She rummaged in her handbag and presented Tat with a Super Star on the spot, which made Mr. and Mrs. Trout beam with pride. It was the first Super Star that anyone in the Trout family had ever received.

"But how on earth did the shoes get in the box and get buried in the first place?"

asked Hetty's mom as everyone else walked around happily in their matching shoes.

Tallulah burst into tears, and Dog looked sorrowful, as if he had just had a very big, juicy bone taken away from him.

"It's all my fault," she sobbed, "and Dog's. He stole the shoes because he loves to chew on them just like a real dog. I didn't have the heart to tell him off. I knew he was only trying to play."

"But why didn't you just give the shoes back?" asked Hetty.

"I was too worried that Dog would get into big trouble and be arrested by the police and flung into the Little Snoring jail," said Tallulah tearfully.

Hetty understood this. In one of her worst moods, and perhaps as a warning as to what might happen to the children if they failed to do their math homework, Miss Green had taken the entire school on a trip to the Little Snoring jail and it had been a horrid place, full of sadness and spiders.

"Is that why you put the shoes in a box and buried them?" asked Hetty gently.

"Yes," said Tallulah. "Dog helped me dig the hole. After we buried them we couldn't remember the spot, so even if we had wanted to find them we couldn't. We are very sorry for all the trouble we caused."

Hetty looked around at all the people on the beach and waved an arm toward them.

"I don't think you should worry too much, Tallulah. Having odd shoes was very inconvenient, but getting them back has made people very pleased."

Dog gave a happy meow, and they joined the others.

But despite all the attention, Tat was feeling a little bit sad inside. He knew that the reward money would only stretch to paying the rent. There would be nothing left over to live on, and in a few months' time his family would be facing financial ruin all over again.

He was thinking about what to do as he and Hetty joined his family and the villagers. Just then the harbormaster appeared by Tat's dad's side.

"Mr. Trout. A word, if you please. I owe you an apology. I'm sorry I took away your job as lighthouse keeper. I thought it was a way to save money. But risking lives is no way to cut costs. I was wrong. If it hadn't been for the bravery and quick thinking of Hetty and your boy, and the resourcefulness of Mrs. Slime, there may have been a disaster. So, Mr. Trout, I'm asking if you will come back to your old job. Mechanization only goes so far. Little Snoring needs a human lighthouse keeper. If you could start tomorrow, the whole village would be in your debt."

"And I'll be able to get out of debt," said Tat's dad with a grin.

When everyone heard the news they all cheered. They decided to have a party to celebrate — and because it was a lovely day and lovely days are always an excuse for a party. The band struck up and they all began to dance.

Merry seagulls

Happy slipper

Cheerful waves

Happy whale

Satisfied starfish

It was a lovely, lovely day, when even ice creams were happy.

Cheerful cloud

Happy sun

Singing sandal

Happy sandcastle

Jolly laughing crab

Pleasured pebbles

Jolly jam sandwich

A barbecue was lit and there were sausages and chicken legs and baked potatoes to eat and games to play, although playing games is tricky when you are not used to wearing matching shoes. Nobody could beat the kangaroos at high jump, but Tat came closest.

A little while later, Tat and Hetty walked down to the shore and looked out toward the horizon. There was no sign of the Ghastly McNastys.

"Maybe we should have just shown the McNastys what was in the box and they would have left us alone," said Tat. "If they had known it

was used shoes and not diamonds and rubies, they wouldn't have been interested."

"Those Ghastly McNastys are so greedy, they would probably have wanted the shoes, too," said Hetty. "Besides, they needed to be taught a lesson, and you did it, Tat."

"Well," said Tat, "we still need to find the real treasure. At least that's the last we'll ever see of the McNasty twins."

"I'm not so sure," said Hetty, who didn't know everything, as it turned out, but who did know a great deal. "I think they might be back."

"I wonder where they are now?" said Tat.

"I don't know," said Hetty, "and it's nice not knowing everything."

(But I do know, and if you would like to, too, please turn over the next page, but only if you are as brave as Tat because it is a truly fearsome sight.)

THE GHASTLY MCNASTYS

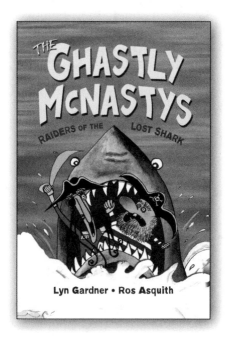

The Ghastly McNastys
return in:

RAIDERS OF THE LOST SHARK

The whole village is excited when a film crew comes to Little Snoring — and none more so than the Ghastly McNasty twins. They plan to storm the set as extras, steal Captain Syd's treasure and show everyone what being a pirate really means!

Only Tat and Hetty can see what the dastardly duo are really up to — but will anyone believe them?

Lyn Gardner is a theater critic for the *Guardian* and goes to the theater five or six times a week, which should leave no time for writing books. But actually she has written several children's books, including the very successful Stage School series. She lives in London, England.

Ros Asquith is a cartoonist for the *Guardian* and has written and illustrated many books. *Letters from an Alien Schoolboy* was shortlisted for the Roald Dahl Funny Prize, and *The Great Big Book of Families*, which she illustrated, won the SLA Information Book Award. She lives in London, England.